CREATURES INFEST LOCAL SCHOOL!

SCIENCE FICTION BY
C.J. HENDERSON

W9-BCS-351

Thompson Middle School
705 W. Main Street
St. Charles, IL 60174

SCHOLASTIC INC.

New York   Toronto   London   Auckland   Sydney
Mexico City   New Delhi   Hong Kong

COVER ILLUSTRATION BY
BRAD WALKER

INTERIOR ILLUSTRATIONS BY
TOM TONKIN

Copyright © 1999 by Scholastic Inc.
All rights reserved. Published by Scholastic Inc.
Printed in the United States of America. 113

ISBN 0-439-05708-6

17   18   19   R   14   13   12

TABLE OF CONTENTS

A teacher is awakened in the middle of the night by some very strange noises.

PROLOGUE

What was that?

Linda Truman sat up in her bed. She didn't make a sound. She was too frightened.

She held the edge of her blanket to her face. In one way, she felt silly. After all, she was an adult. She was a respected social studies teacher at one of New England's finest private schools.

She was young, but she was supposed to set an example. She wasn't supposed to be scared by noises in the night.

Well, I am, okay? she thought. *I am scared.*

Like the other teachers and students, Linda slept in a dorm. She'd been hearing these noises every other night for weeks. So had her students. Now, she was hearing the noises again. Something was moving around downstairs in the library.

That "something" was not supposed to be there.

Linda did not want to get out of bed. She wanted to close her eyes and go back to sleep.

But she knew she couldn't. She had to find out what the noise was. She had to do it for the sake of the kids. She had to make sure they were safe.

What on earth could those noises be?

It wasn't thieves. Nothing had ever been taken from the school. It wasn't animals. No one had found a trace of fur or feathers. There had been no scratch marks. No evidence hinted that an animal had been inside.

Linda got out of bed. She got up even though she was still very afraid. She was determined to find out what was moving around in the library.

She slipped on her bathrobe and slippers. She went out into the hall. She walked toward the stairs. The strange noises grew louder and louder. Her mind buzzed with a million warnings.

You should have a light, she thought. *You should have a weapon. You should put your shoes on. You shouldn't go down there. You're going to get killed. You should call the police.*

"Oh, just shut up and go downstairs," she told herself aloud. Immediately, the noises stopped.

You should keep quiet, she thought.

Linda knew she had just made a big mistake. Now, whatever was downstairs knew that someone was awake. It knew someone was walking around. It knew someone was looking for it.

Linda's curiosity turned to cold fear.

She turned around carefully. She pulled her robe tight. Then she started back to her room.

She was too late.

The hair on the back of Linda's neck began to itch. Then it froze. The noises were moving. They were crossing the great stone floor. Now they were climbing the stairs.

Linda ran. She knew what the noises were now. They were tapping claws. And they were terrible, frightening whispers.

Linda was halfway back to her room when the sounds reached the top of the stairs. She tried to run faster. Her fuzzy slippers began to slide from her feet. She tried to keep running without losing her slippers. She couldn't.

Linda fell. First she hit the wall, then the floor. Her head struck the wall hard. Her finger bent backward. She cried out in pain.

The noises were very close now. Terrified, the teacher turned to see what was getting so close to her. She saw—and she wished that she hadn't.

Linda's mouth hung open. She tried to stand. She tried to scream. Ugly, tiny figures were coming toward her. They were hairy, bent things with skinny arms and pointed ears. They had hateful faces and red, glowing eyes.

There were three of them or five or . . .

There were eight of them.

They came closer—and closer. Linda looked into the shining eyes of the one nearest to her. She looked into all their eyes at once. They grew even closer. She felt the warmth of the nearest one's breath. She smelled the dripping heat of it.

Then she screamed.

Where do you think these creatures came from? Are they dangerous?

Meanwhile, Jack McCay, monster hunter, prepares to meet the beast of Lake Champlain.

CHAPTER 1

"The grapes and fish heads aren't working."

Frank the sailor looked out at the man hanging over the front of the boat. Frank shouted back, "What do you want to try next?"

"Give me the cabbage."

The sailor dug through a cooler filled with vegetables, fruit, fish, and raw meat. Ed, the boat's mechanic, came up to him.

"Frank, who is that guy, anyway?"

"He's Jack McCay, man," whispered Frank. "He's a reporter—you know, the monster hunter."

Ed just stared.

"He's on TV sometimes," Frank said. "He researches the world's mysteries."

"Oh," Ed said. "He must be here looking for Champ, right?"

Frank nodded. Champ was the only thing that would bring a monster hunter to Lake Champlain. For centuries, there had been stories of a giant creature living in the lake. An explorer named Samuel de Champlain had been the first to sight the beast. That had been back in 1609. The reports hadn't stopped coming since then.

Frank handed the cabbage to McCay. "Do you really think there could be a monster in this lake?"

"Sure, it's a cold, freshwater lake. All the well-known lake creatures come from them. Plus, it's big. It's 100 miles long and 13 miles across. It's over 400 feet deep. That gives a monster plenty of room to hide."

McCay fumbled with the head of cabbage. He tore it in half. He threw the pieces over the side. Then his hands went back to his camera.

The boat circled slowly. It had been circling like that for the past two weeks.

McCay stared out over the water. He wanted to see if anything would show any interest in the floating cabbage leaves. He saw a slight disturbance off to his right. He turned to Frank. "What do you make of those ripples over there?"

"I don't know. Schools of fish *definitely* don't move like that."

Jack McCay grew excited. His grip on his camera tightened. He asked Frank to get them closer to the ripples. The sailor went back to talk to the captain. At the same time, McCay inched his way to the front of the boat. He was excited and more than a little scared.

"Come on, Champ, old boy," he whispered. He looked at his watch and grew more nervous. "Be out there, will you? I really need you to be there."

Slowly, the boat moved toward the strange ripples in the water. McCay hung onto the ship's rail with one hand. He held his camera with the other. The weird waves did not disappear. In fact, they grew larger.

"This is it," shouted the reporter. "For crying out loud—this is it!"

McCay kept one hand on the rail. He worked his video camera with the other. He turned it toward the water carefully. The boat slowed down. Tension filled the air. A horrible dark shadow began to move up toward the water's surface. The ripples grew even wilder.

"Is that an eye?" Frank asked the captain.

"An eye?" repeated the captain. "Are those jaws I see? Open jaws?"

McCay could hear the men. He saw what they saw. He could make out the same huge eye. He could see the same jaws.

"Now I got you, Champ," he said.

McCay let go of the rail. He planted his feet as firmly as he could. Then he smiled and focused his camera. A large, snake-like head looked up from beneath the water. It saw him. McCay's finger found the record button. Tape started flowing.

Suddenly there was a flash of movement. The water exploded. Huge waves sprayed in all directions. The worst of them blasted the boat.

"Captain!"

Frank cried out as a wall of water crashed against the boat. He saw McCay's arms fly upward. Then the reporter's video camera bounced against the deck. Its shattered pieces were scattered across the water. There was no sign of the owner.

Jack McCay was gone.

Could it be that after a long and freaky career, Jack McCay is finally all washed up?

CHAPTER **2**

Luckily, McCay wasn't gone for long. The sailors soon spotted him. They fished him out of the lake before he could drown. Then they took him back to shore. He walked the half-mile to his hotel still soaking wet. He went into his room and stared at the remains of his video camera.

"A lot of good this does me!"

McCay threw the pieces of his camera across his hotel room. He was angry. He had been so close, he thought. Getting footage of Champ would have been a big story—*the biggest.*

"More than that," McCay muttered to himself. "It would have paid a lot of bills."

Yet all he'd ended up with was a broken camera and a soaking wet suit. Jack McCay was not happy. He was also not certain what he was going to do next. Like many people, he lived from paycheck to paycheck. His work wasn't steady. Sometimes, like now, it was a long time between checks.

McCay had studied the records on Champ carefully. He had noticed a pattern to the creature's sightings. He was certain that the beast would be feeding near Port Henry, in New York, during the first two weeks of that month.

He had taken all his cash and found a place to stay in town. He had rented a boat and crew. For two weeks he had tried to find Champ. Now, on the last day he could afford to stay in town, he had finally located the monster. He had come so close, so very close. . . .

"But," he said sourly, "close doesn't cut it."

He had no more money left. He could no longer rent the captain's boat. He couldn't afford his room for another day. He couldn't even afford dinner.

He began to go through the mail that had piled up for him at the hotel. For the past week, he had been practically living on the boat with Frank and the captain. "I'd better find something to do in this stack," he said, "or I'm really in trouble."

McCay opened letter after letter. The first was from an editor at a magazine called *Stranger Than Truth*. He needed a story for the October issue. Did McCay have anything for him? The producer of the TV series *Challenge of the Unknown* needed a piece for the last show of the season. Did McCay have something?

"No," McCay said in a loud, angry voice. "No, no, no!"

Then he opened the only envelope left in the pile. He'd saved it for last because he didn't recognize the return address. It had been sent from some small school in New England.

Maybe they wanted him to be a guest speaker. Probably they wanted some kind of donation. He read the letter anyway.

Minutes later, he was wringing out his soaking socks and packing his bags. He also made a call to the train station. He wanted to see if he could trade his ticket to Chicago for one to New England.

What do you think the small school in New England wants from Jack McCay?

Back at Linda Truman's school, everyone is in a big uproar about some little pests.

CHAPTER 3

"Ms. Truman, be reasonable."

Linda Truman stared at Boyd Dexter, the principal of her school. His bald head was shining with sweat. She knew why he was sweating. He was scared. Linda didn't care.

The young teacher was not happy. She couldn't believe that the principal was saying what he was saying. On the other hand, what else would he say?

"I *am* being reasonable!" She looked at the school officials gathered around the table.

"Oh, really, Linda," said Ms. Bloathistle. She was the principal's adviser. "Little creatures, glowing claws . . . You can't be serious."

"Their eyes were glowing, not their claws. And you bet I'm serious. I saw them. They're here. Don't you see what that means? We're responsible for the students, you know."

"We don't need a lecture about our responsibilities from you," sniffed Ms. Bloathistle.

"No?" asked Linda. "Well, you certainly need a lecture from *someone*."

"Ms. Truman, you're the laughing-stock of the school," Mr. Dexter said.

Linda tried to get her temper under control. "I know what's going on here," she said, lowering her voice. "You're afraid of looking silly. So you're trying to cover up the situation."

"Now, Linda . . ."

"It's true. You don't care if monsters run through the kids' dorms at night. All you care about is your image. But what's going to happen to that image when one of those things attacks a student? How embarrassing will it be when someone ends up in the hospital. . . ."

"Linda, hold on a minute!"

". . . Or maybe in their grave!" Linda continued.

"Ms. Truman," huffed Ms. Bloathistle. Her round face went red. "You're asking to be fired."

"And you're asking for a lawsuit."

Ms. Bloathistle's eyes grew wide. She began to stammer. So did the principal. So did the others at the table. They had thought they could frighten Linda with the threat of losing her job.

They'd been wrong. The things in the hall had scared Linda more than anything in her life. The threat of being fired didn't frighten her at all.

On the other hand, *her* threat to sue the school had the school officials *very* scared. The principal could just picture what would happen. He could see the reporters swarming over the school. He could imagine the news reports. He could just hear the late-night comedians making jokes. He could already picture people all across the country laughing at his school—and at him. He could also see the school's board firing him for it all.

Still, he thought, what if she's right? What if one of the students *did* get hurt? What if monsters really *were* roaming the campus?

The principal pushed the idea out of his head. It was ridiculous. Still, he had a big problem.

Linda was still shouting at Ms. Bloathistle. Ms. Bloathistle was screaming back. The rest of the school staff looked scared and angry.

Dexter ducked under the table as a book flew through the air. He thought Ms. Bloathistle had thrown it. He didn't know for sure. He thought he'd take a peek to see what was happening. He put his head up as another book followed the first.

He couldn't believe it. Everyone was screaming at each other. They were throwing things and shaking their fists. What would happen next?

That's when Jack McCay walked through the doors of the meeting room.

Jack McCay and Linda Truman now begin their investigation into the school's creepy mystery.

CHAPTER 4

Less than an hour later, Linda was taking McCay across the school grounds. His suitcase was still in his hand. His wet socks were sticking out of his jacket pocket. He looked around and studied everything around him.

"I still can't believe that they're letting you investigate," Linda said.

McCay smiled. "Come on now, Ms. Truman. Think about the way we set things up. They would have been crazy not to go for it."

"I don't understand."

"They only agreed to let me investigate— quietly. You agreed to resign—without a lawsuit— if I didn't find anything."

"But if there are monsters, you get to tell the full story," Linda said. "How did you manage that?"

"That part is the simplest. They don't want to believe in monsters. They'd prefer to think you're nuts. So the trick was getting you to agree to quit if there were no monsters."

Just then a group of students came into view. They ran straight to Linda. They stared at McCay.

"See?" shouted one boy. "I told you it was him."

"You're Jack McCay, the monster hunter, aren't you?" asked the girl. "You're here to get rid of those things Ms. Truman saw. Aren't you?"

"Now, kids," said Linda. "Mr. McCay will be busy for quite some time. We can't—"

McCay interrupted her. "Okay if I call you Linda?" he asked.

"Sure," she said.

"Linda, trust me on this one." He turned to the students. "Look here. I need you to do me a favor."

"You got it!" shouted the first boy.

"I want you to go find every kid who's seen or heard these creatures," said McCay. "Get them all to the library in, say, 15 minutes?"

The students tore off in different directions, shouting for their friends. McCay watched them run across the school's wide yard. Smiling, he told Linda, "Now we're getting somewhere."

How should Jack and Linda go
about investigating the creatures?

The students shed some light on the situation, and Jack and Linda get closer to the truth.

CHAPTER 5

McCay had finished asking the students about the creatures. He was walking around the library, studying the display cases that lined the room. "What is all this stuff, anyway?" he asked one of the kids.

"Well, these displays show recent archeological finds," one boy answered. "All these artifacts were discovered in the caves beneath the school."

"Yeah, but what are they?" McCay asked. "I see arrowheads and pottery and the usual stuff. What makes any of this load so special?"

"Oh, it's their age," another kid answered. "They're the oldest things that have ever been found in New England."

McCay's left eyebrow shot upward. "Which case holds the oldest pieces?"

"The really old pieces are still in the lab. Scientists are still trying to confirm their age."

"That's too bad," said the reporter. He opened

his suitcase. "They would have made good shots for an article. Still, I can get some pictures of the hall. My video recorder was destroyed on Lake Champlain, but I still have 'Old Faithful' here."

McCay pulled an extremely old camera from his suitcase. "Say hello to 'Baby.' I got my first picture of the Flatwoods Monster with her."

"The Flatwoods Monster?" asked one student.

"Haven't you heard about that?" McCay was about to tell the tale of his first big story.

Then the the late bell sounded.

"Oops," said Linda. "Okay, kids, no more stories. Run off to bed, everybody."

The students groaned. They wanted to keep talking with McCay. But Linda was firm. Rules were rules.

After the students left, Linda turned to McCay. "Well, the kids weren't very helpful about the creatures, were they?" she said.

"Not helpful?" The shock in McCay's voice was genuine. "They told us tons."

"They didn't tell you any more than I did. I'm the only one who's actually seen anything."

"They told us a lot. First, we found out that this building is the only place the strange creatures have visited. Second, we learned that they've only heard things down here—in the library. That's what we in the business call a 'localized phenomenon.'"

McCay paused. "Hey, that reminds me," he said. "You were interrupted earlier. You never finished telling me how you got away from those things."

"Well, I screamed," said Linda. "Then everyone started turning on lights and pouring into the hallway. I'm ashamed to admit that I was so afraid I closed my eyes. I never saw what happened to the monsters. They just disappeared."

"Don't be embarrassed," said McCay. He lined up a shot of a display case. "It happens all the time. I almost fainted when I saw my first monster."

Linda smiled. She liked Jack McCay. First, he was the only person besides the kids who believed her. Second, he was smart and funny. He saw things differently than most people.

Linda walked over to the display case. She wanted to look at the objects through the reporter's eyes.

Then, suddenly, Linda heard something. Her heart began beating very fast. The noise sounded very much like tapping claws and terrible, frightening whispers.

After a moment, Jack McCay heard it as well.

What's that tapping? McCay tries to figure out what's making that annoying noise.

CHAPTER 6

"Is that what I think it is?" asked the reporter. Suddenly Jack McCay was very excited.

"It is," Linda assured him. She shuddered as she added, "I'll never forget that sound."

McCay closed his eyes. "Where do you think it's coming from?" he asked her.

She listened a moment. "Upstairs," she said.

"What's the fastest way up there?" McCay asked. Then he took a good look at Linda. "Hey, are you okay? You're not too scared, are you?"

Linda took a breath. She shook her head "no."

McCay smiled. His picked up his camera and grabbed Linda's arm. "Lead on, fair lady. We've got some monsters to snag!"

Linda led McCay to the stairs. They climbed to the top floor and looked around. The tapping sounds were still coming from above them.

"They must be in the attic." Linda pointed to a small door at the end of the hall. "That doorway leads to the attic stairs," she said.

"Do me a favor and stay here," McCay said. "I may need you to call for help." He walked over to the door and pulled. It opened with a loud creak. McCay began climbing the narrow stairs.

Moments later he stuck his head up into the attic. He looked around. He didn't see anything except dusty crates and stacks of old furniture. He closed his eyes and began to listen carefully. After a moment, he called down to Linda.

"They're not in the attic," he told her. "They're outside—on the roof."

"What are they doing out there?" she asked.

"I don't know," answered McCay. "I'd like to go ask them. Is there a way out there from here?"

"There's a small door at the far end of the attic. It's how the janitors get to the gutters."

"That sounds good," said McCay.

Linda stood in the hallway below. Kids began to come out of their rooms to see what was going on. Everyone stared upward into the dark attic. They listened to the horrible tapping noises. They waited for something to happen.

They didn't have to wait long.

Should McCay go out on the roof?

Jack McCay has some close encounters with some very strange—and angry—creatures.

CHAPTER 7

McCay pulled himself out onto the roof. He was grateful that there was a clear sky and an almost full moon.

At least I can see where I'm going, he thought.

Slowly, the reporter inched his way along the roof. He could still hear the tapping sounds. They couldn't be anything but claws scraping against the slate tiles of the roof.

He moved forward. The tapping seemed to come from a different direction. He moved again. The tapping seemed to come from somewhere else. Why did the things keep moving around? What could they be doing, he wondered. Then, suddenly, he knew.

They're surrounding you, you dope!

He tried to remember the way back to the little attic door. The old dormitory roof was a maze of chimneys. He had been so excited to catch up with the monsters that he hadn't thought of anything else. Now, the things were closing in on him!

Oh great, he thought. *Now what do I do?*

Louder noises sprang up directly in front of him. They were coming right at him. McCay backed up further and further. Suddenly, he was at the edge of the roof.

Oh, man, he thought. *I didn't bring anything with me except my camera.*

Then the first monster turned the corner. It was a dark and hairy creature only a little over two feet tall. Even in the dark, McCay could see that Linda had described the things perfectly. Three more figures came into view. They were all like the first—bent things with skinny arms and pointed ears. They had sharp claws, dripping, pointed teeth, and red, glowing eyes.

A noise made the reporter look over his shoulder. Two more were coming from the other direction. He turned back toward another noise. A sixth was coming straight over the gable in front of him. A seventh was right behind that one.

They've got me, McCay realized.

Well, the reporter told himself, *I came up here for some pictures. I might as well get some.*

His finger came down on the shutter release. The camera's lens tripped. The flash exploded.

Then the screaming began.

26

Linda Truman has a blindingly bright insight about the creatures.

CHAPTER 8

Jack McCay couldn't believe his eyes. His attackers—the trolls, the creatures—were gone! They had completely disappeared!

He carefully made his way back to the door of the attic. Linda and her students were calling to him. He shouted back that he was okay.

"They ran away," Jack told Linda.

"What do you mean, ran away?" Linda asked.

"I'm telling you, Linda," McCay answered as he climbed down the attic stairs. "They just ran away. It was really strange. They had me surrounded. Then I decided to take their pictures."

Linda simply stared at first. "You decided to take their pictures? Why?" she asked.

"I figured maybe someone would find my camera. That way at least you'd have proof they existed—even if something happened to me. But when the flash lit up, they all ran shrieking into the night."

Suddenly Linda shouted, "That's it!"

"What's it?"

"Could you repeat what you just said, Jack?" Linda asked.

"I said that I wanted you to have proof that the creatures existed," McCay said.

"No, after that. What did you say after that?" Linda said.

"When the flash went off, the creatures took off, too," Jack said.

Linda smiled, "Exactly. *They ran away from the flash because they can't stand light!*"

McCay thought for a moment. He realized that Linda had to be right. The things had run away and left Linda alone when people started turning on lights. They also had run from his camera's flash. In fact, they had not just run. They had seemed almost physically wounded.

At the time, McCay had not thought about their response. He had been too busy trying to escape.

Now the puzzle pieces were suddenly falling into place.

"Good grief," shouted the reporter. "I know what's going on!"

"What? What?!" the students demanded.

"I can't take the time to explain now," he told them. "So you're going to have to trust me. And you have to do exactly as I say. I have a pretty good idea what these things are. And they're probably dangerous."

"What do you want us to do?" asked a boy.

"Stay in your rooms. Sleep with the lights on. Keep flashlights with you. If you see the little creeps, shine your lights in their eyes. Ms. Truman and I will try to find them by morning. We'll be back with the whole story."

"Where are you going?" asked another student.

McCay looked the girl straight in the eye. He answered in a deadly serious voice.

"We're going on a journey to the center of the earth."

Why do you think that McCay would look for these creatures in the center of the earth?

According to many cultures, McCay tells Linda, little people actually live in the center of the earth.

CHAPTER 9

"Oh, my gosh," said Linda. "You were right."

She and McCay stood at the entrance to a cave a few hundred feet away from where the ancient artifacts had been found. Linda's flashlight lit up the ground in front of the entrance. Tiny footprints were everywhere.

McCay checked his camera. "It just came together for me. You had said that the little guys ran away when the lights came on. Then they ran away from the camera flash. Put that together with everything else. It just makes sense."

"Put it together with what else?" asked Linda. They started walking into the cave.

"You said the oldest artifacts were recent discoveries. Then the little guys showed up right after they were taken from the caves. It's classic."

"I don't know what you mean."

"Oh, come on," said McCay. "You've seen mummy movies, haven't you? You take something out of the tomb. Then something else comes out of the tomb to get it back."

"So you think that these little people live underground? You think that they want their artifacts back?" Linda beamed her flashlight around the narrow cave.

"Right," McCay said.

"But how could there be creatures living underground?" Linda asked.

"You've never heard of the 'Hollow Earth' theories?" asked McCay.

Linda shook her head.

"I'm surprised. Every country in the world has legends about it."

"They do?"

"I'll tell you about it while we look around."

McCay and Linda started making their way through the caves.

"All these stories involve creatures who live in unknown lands inside the earth," McCay began.

"Olaf Jansen, a sailor from Norway, claimed he entered the Hollow Earth through an opening at the North Pole. Strangely enough, Admiral Richard Byrd, who later explored the North Pole, claimed there was an opening there as well. What's more, some religions also describe communities at the center of the earth."

"That's unbelievable," Linda said.

"It can't all be true," McCay agreed. "Still, so many people believe the same thing. Don't you think there has to be something to it?"

"You mean like UFOs?" asked Linda.

"It's funny you would mention that. Believe it or not, a lot of people think that UFOs are from the Hollow Earth."

"Oh, please," Linda laughed. "Don't tell me you believe that."

"Well, no," answered McCay.

"Well, all I know is—"

Linda suddenly stopped talking. McCay understood why. He had heard the same thing she had. It was coming from around the bend. It was a noise they had both heard before—the sound of tapping claws and terrible, frightening whispers.

Linda could feel her heart beating faster. McCay was not scared. After all, the things ran away from light. How much trouble could they be?

No, Jack McCay was ready for this batch of monsters. He knew their weakness. He had his camera. He had a flashlight. He knew he would have no trouble sending them running.

This time, thought the reporter, I win.

Then he heard the boulder falling from above.

Linda and Jack seem to have found an underground land—but will they ever surface?

CHAPTER **10**

BAM! The boulder smashed into the cave wall just above their heads! Splinters from the enormous rock filled the air.

"Linda!" McCay leaped across the space that separated him from Linda. He knocked her backward. Seconds later, three more boulders crashed against the spot where she had been. More jagged pieces of rock flew through the cavern. The rocks slammed against everything, including McCay and Linda—and their flashlights.

Nuts, thought the reporter. He tried his flashlight. He hoped that the sound he had heard had not been breaking glass.

It had been. The flashlight didn't work. He told Linda to try hers. She did. It didn't work either.

"What'll we do now?" she asked.

"Move!" shouted McCay. Another boulder came crashing down toward them. They moved out of the way with just a second to spare. They stood with their backs to the cave wall. Both of them were choking on the dust filling the cave. McCay forced himself to stop coughing. Then he heard the tapping once more.

"They're moving in on us," he whispered to Linda. The pair stood in the darkness. They could barely see each other. They could not yet see the tiny monsters. They could only hear the things' sharp, curved claws clicking against the cavern's stone floor.

"I'm sorry I got you into this, Jack," Linda said.

"You got me into this?" McCay said. "No way. You invited me, that's true, but I came on my own."

McCay gripped Linda's arm. He knew that their situation didn't look good. An attack was surely coming, and they had no weapons. They both had broken flashlights. Then he remembered something. He pulled his camera from his coat.

"Come on, Baby," he whispered to it. He aimed it in the general direction of the approaching tapping. "Just get us out of this one last scrape."

McCay prepared his camera. In the distance, the tiny creatures began to chant.

"Twilger. Twilger. Twilger. Twilger. Twilger…"

"What's that all about?" asked Linda.

McCay didn't have time to answer. A monster came into view. He was much taller than the others—some three feet in height. He was thick with muscles and covered in long, dark hair. The thing drew closer and closer to them.

Linda pulled at McCay's sleeve. "That one—he must be . . . be this . . . 'Twilger.'"

McCay nodded, whispering back, "Stop shaking my arm. I want to try and get his picture when I use the flash."

Linda let go of McCay's arm. "Do you think we can get out of this?" she asked.

"I don't know, Linda," answered McCay honestly. "I'll do whatever I can."

McCay was just about to set off his flash. Then the monster the others called Twilger stopped ten feet from where they stood.

"You want to get out of this, tall guy?" the monster said. "Give us back our stuff!"

What *stuff* do you think the Twilger creature is talking about?

Linda and Jack get a short course in the little creatures' long history.

CHAPTER **11**

Jack McCay and Linda Truman sat on a stone next to the creature called Twilger. The rest of his people stood around them with spears and stone axes. Both McCay and Linda were uncomfortable. So far, however, they had not been harmed.

So far.

They had just heard the tale of how the first "Old Ones," as Twilger's people called themselves, had come to America. They had crossed the Atlantic nearly 1,000 years earlier. They had come with explorer Leif Eriksson and his Vikings. That was 500 years before Christopher Columbus was even born.

Linda looked around the cave. Her eyes had adjusted to the dark. In one corner, she saw hundreds of treasures that the Old Ones had collected over the centuries.

A nearly perfect dragon-headed Viking ship caught her eye. She stared at it for a moment.

"So," said Twilger. "What's next? You have to help us get our stuff back—or *you're* history."

McCay stalled. "First, let me see if I understand all this. Your people came from Europe with the explorers from Scandinavia. They discovered Nova Scotia—"

"They discovered what?" asked Twilger. He looked confused.

"Up north," answered McCay. "Canada."

"The Vikings called it 'Vineland,'" said Linda.

"Oh, yeah, Vineland," said Twilger. "Why didn't you say so?"

"Thanks, Linda," whispered McCay. Then he turned back to Twilger. "Your people were the inspiration for all the legends about trolls and fairies—right?"

"Right," agreed Twilger.

"You're one of the tribes of cave dwellers who have hidden underground for hundreds and hundreds of years."

"Yup," said Twilger.

"Well, it seems to me that you have a bigger problem than getting your stuff back."

"Like what?" asked Twilger.

"The surface scientists have found some of your artifacts. If you steal them back, they'll come here looking for them. They'll find you."

"Well . . ." Twilger looked disturbed.

"In fact, they may be looking around here anyway," McCay said.

"I hope not," said Twilger. "That would really mess us up."

"Why?" Linda asked.

"We live pretty simply down here," Twilger said. "We still use flint to light our fires. Introducing the Old Ones to VCRs, video games, and the Internet would be a shock. It would destroy our culture."

"Still," said Linda, "your people seem to know everything about the surface."

"I know about the surface—only me. That's my job," answered Twilger. "One member of every tribe learns the main surface language in any area. I keep up with everything going on outside. Right now the elders are pretty upset about you 'Talls' finding us. We're too proud to perform as freaks, you know."

"So," asked Linda, "what's your solution?" She listened as Twilger and the elders talked in some unknown language.

"The elders say we should just kill you two. Then we'd be done with it. That way, you couldn't bring anyone else back here."

McCay's smile faded. Linda's face went pale.

Linda swallowed hard and started talking before any of the Old Ones could make a move. "That's not such a great solution," she said. "If we disappear, people will come looking for us. You don't want that."

Twilger shook his head.

"I might have an idea that could solve this problem a little better," said Linda.

"Tell us about it," said Twilger.

Linda stared out into the sea of glowing eyes and sharp spears. Then she glanced at the old Viking ship once more.

"Here's my idea . . ."

Back at the school, a very old ship docks at a brand new port.

CHAPTER 12

BAAADDDAAAA-WWHHHOOOOMMMM!

The crashing noise shook the whole school. Plates rattled in the kitchen. Chalk bounced off the blackboards. Leaves fell off the trees. All the car alarms went off for a mile around. People stopped whatever they were doing. Everything totally stopped.

It simply had to.

"What in the world was that?"

"I don't know."

Principal Dexter and Ms. Bloathistle picked themselves up off the floor. They were both very confused. They looked around the office at all the pictures hanging sideways. They looked at each other. Then they ran out of the office.

Teachers and students poured out of all the other buildings. So did the cafeteria workers and the janitors. Everyone had heard the thundering noise. They all wanted to see what had happened.

43

They all rushed to the area where the noise had come from.

They couldn't believe their eyes.

"Everyone calm down," shouted Mr. Dexter. "Calm down. Let me through! You must let me through, everyone!"

The principal made his way to the front of the crowd. He finally reached the edge of the group. He couldn't believe what he was seeing.

"How? What? Why? When—" he stammered.

Everyone was staring at a huge hole in the lawn. Finally the dust stopped pouring out of it. Everyone looked down and saw . . .

"Ms. Truman! Mr. McCay!"

"Hey, Dexter, old boy," shouted the reporter. "I'm glad to see you. Get us out of here. Man, do we have a story for you!"

Dexter looked at all the ruined property. He wondered if the board would blame him for it. He wondered if he would lose his job.

Then he saw a dragon's head towering behind McCay. It was a very, very old dragon's head attached to a very, very old ship.

Suddenly, Boyd Dexter was no longer worried.

Where did the dragon ship come from?

Linda explains her brilliant idea—and considers a new career.

EPILOGUE

"Truman," said McCay the next day as he packed his bag. "You were right. The school bought that Viking ship deal without a question."

"Well, Jack," answered the teacher modestly. "I have to admit it was a pretty good idea."

"Pretty good idea?" McCay said. "I'd call it genius. We promise the Old Ones that we'll trade all those artifacts in the library for one gigantic Viking ship. We also promise not to breathe a word about them. No one will come looking for them."

"And of course school officials are more than happy never to mention the creatures again," said Linda. "They didn't want the publicity the monster story would bring. Meanwhile, they love the publicity about a Viking ship discovered right on school grounds. They were happy that all they had to do was 'misplace' the artifacts in the library."

"Presto—everyone is happy," McCay said,

admiringly. "It's perfect. I just have one question. How did you ever recognize that old Viking ship?"

"I'm a social studies teacher, remember? I look at pictures of Viking ships in the textbook every September. Page 56."

"I love it," McCay said with a smile.

"I'm just sorry you didn't get that story you needed," Linda said.

"Are you crazy, Truman?" the reporter exclaimed. "The Viking ship is my story. I've already closed a deal with *Challenge of the Unknown*. Two magazines and four different radio shows want it, too. I've got the rent covered for the next five years."

McCay patted his camera. Then he placed it in his bag between his socks and underwear.

"There you go, Baby," he told it. "You're all ready for the drive home."

The reporter packed a couple of shirts on top of his camera and closed his bag. Then he and Linda headed outside to his rental car.

A lot of the kids crowded around. The students all had questions about the caves. What other things had the two of them seen underground? Finally, the bell for the first class rang.

"All right," said Linda. "All of you, get going."

Then Linda turned to McCay. "I have to go, too.

I just want to say thank you for the adventure."

"Hey, I couldn't have done it without you. And besides, I got a story."

"And you're sure that the Viking ship is a big enough story for you?" Linda asked.

"Definitely," Jack responded.

"What about the tribes of little people living underground all over the world?" Linda asked. "We know now that trolls and elves are real. Wouldn't that be the biggest story of the century?"

"Hey, what can I say?" asked the reporter. He flashed Linda a smile. "We gave the Old Ones our word. They let us go. They gave up one of their most precious relics for us. The least we can do is keep our promise."

"Besides," he went on. "They're sending one of their people into the outside world with me. Twilger is going to keep tabs on me. He'll make sure I don't say anything."

Linda laughed. "It's pretty obvious he's dying to get out into the world."

Suddenly, a car stopped sharply in front of them, screeching its tires. The driver was sitting on top of four phone books. He was no more than three feet tall. His long hair was slicked down under a ton of grease. He was wearing a bright Hawaiian shirt. He wore the thickest, heaviest sunglasses that they had ever seen.

The little man beeped the car's horn long and loud. Then he shouted at McCay. "Come on, Jack, *Maybe It's True* wants us in Tennessee by Tuesday to investigate that UFO landing! We've got to go!"

McCay smiled at Twilger and grabbed his bag. He threw it into the car and jumped into the passenger seat. Then he turned to Linda. "I'll send you a postcard from Nashville, Truman."

Linda watched as the reporter and his new partner headed down the driveway. She wondered what they would find.

She started off for her first class. She promised herself she would start reading the newspapers— every single day. Then she thought . . .

Why just read them?

The idea startled her. Linda Truman had spent her whole life being quiet and secure. She had never made any trouble. She had never even done anything exciting—until she met Jack McCay.

She thought about the rest of her life. She saw herself teaching in her quiet little school. She saw herself never risking her life as she had the night before. She saw herself with Mr. Dexter and Ms. Bloathistle as her bosses—forever.

She saw herself never seeing Jack McCay again.

"No," she said aloud. "I definitely should have gone with them."

"Yeah," came Twilger's voice. "That's what Jack says."

Linda turned. The rental car was back. Twilger was at the wheel. The passenger door was open.

She saw adventure and excitement waiting for her there. She saw a life roaming the globe, searching for mystery and monsters. Then she looked into Jack's eyes. She looked long and hard. She saw that Jack McCay no longer wanted to do all that if she wasn't there to help him.

She smiled. He smiled back. Twilger rolled his eyes. She ran into the car. And she never looked back.

They all investigated happily ever after.

Do you think that Linda Truman will like her new career?

DID YOU LIKE THIS BOOK?

Here are two other READ 180 Paperbacks that you might like to read.

VISITORS

Why are all the adults in Harley Hills acting so strangely? Have they been taken over by aliens?!

BY RODMAN PHILBRICK AND LYNN HARNETT

NIGHT HUNTERS

Students in the future use virtual reality to get into the heads of animals that are on the hunt— and animals that are hunted!

BY DAVE LUCKETT

GLOSSARY

archeological   having to do with archeology, the study of the past. Archeology is done by digging up and examining old objects and buildings.

artifacts   objects made by humans, especially tools or weapons, used in the past

centuries   periods of one hundred years

dorm   short for dormitory

dormitory   a building with many rooms for sleeping

epilogue   a short piece of writing added to the end of a play, story, or poem

flint   a hard stone that makes sparks when steel is struck against it

fumbled   handled clumsily

lawsuit   a legal action or case brought against a person or a group in a court of law

localized	limited to one area
phenomenon	an event; usually something very remarkable
prologue	a short piece of writing that introduces a play, story, or poem
publicity	information that is told to the public
stammer	to speak in an unsure way